Parents and Caregivers,

Stone Arch Readers are designed to provide
experiences, as well as opportunities to develop vocabulary,
literacy skills, and comprehension. Here are a few ways to
support your beginning reader:

- Talk with your child about the ideas addressed in the story.

- Discuss each illustration, mentioning the characters, where
  they are, and what they are doing.

- Read with expression, pointing to each word. You may want to
  read the whole story through and then revisit parts of the story
  to ensure that the meanings of words or phrases are understood.

- Talk about why the character did what he or she did and what
  your child would do in that situation.

- Help your child connect with characters and events in the story.

Remember, reading with your child should be fun, not forced.
Each moment spent reading with your child is a priceless
investment in his or her literacy life.

Gail Saunders-Smith, Ph.D.

STONE ARCH READERS

are published by Stone Arch Books, a Capstone Imprint
1710 Roe Crest Drive
North Mankato, Minnesota 56003
www.capstonepub.com

Library of Congress Cataloging-in-Publication Data is available on the
Library of Congress website.
ISBN: 978-1-4342-2005-9 (library binding)
ISBN: 978-1-4342-2789-8 (paperback)

Summary: Gary the lizard is excited for his first day of school.

Reading Consultants:
Gail Saunders-Smith, Ph.D.
Melinda Melton Crow, M.Ed.
Laurie K. Holland, Media Specialist

Art Director/Designer: Kay Fraser
Production Specialist: Michelle Biedscheid

illustrated by Andy Rowland

Little Lizard's
FIRST DAY

by Melinda
Melton Crow

STONE ARCH BOOKS
a capstone imprint

This is Dad Lizard
This is Mom Lizard.
This is Gary Lizard.

Gary was asleep.

"Wake up, Gary," said Mom.

"Today is your first day
of school," said Dad.

11

"Oh boy!" said Gary.

13

"I am going to school today!"
said Gary.

"Here are your clothes,"
said Mom.

"Here is your backpack,"
said Dad.

"Here is my lunch,"
said Gary.

"I am ready!" said Gary.

"First you have to eat,"
said Mom.

"I am hungry," said Gary.

"One more thing," said Dad.

"Now I am ready. Goodbye!"
said Gary.

STORY WORDS

lizard	school	lunch
Gary	clothes	ready
asleep	backpack	goodbye

Total Word Count: 88

Little Lizard's BOOKSTORE

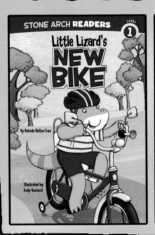

4 NEW TITLES